NOT THAT NICE

Michelle D. Rayford

Barrington Drive Publishing Company

COLUMBIA, SOUTH CAROLINA

Michelle D. Rayford/Barrington Drive Publishing Company
4611 Hard Scrabble Road, Suite 109 #340
Columbia, SC 29229
www.barringtondrivepublishing.com

Publisher's Note: This is a work of fiction. Names, characters, places, and incidents are a product of the author's imagination and are used fictitiously and are not to be construed as real. Locales and public names are sometimes used for atmospheric purposes. Any resemblance to actual people, living or dead, or to businesses, companies, events, organizations, institutions, or locales is completely coincidental.

Book Layout © 2017 BookDesignTemplates.com
Book Cover Design: Lissa Woodson – www.naleighnakai.com

Not That Nice/ Michelle D. Rayford -- 1st ed.
ISBN 978-0-9997303-5-5

For My Girls – Still chasing the dream!

CONTENTS

HERE AND NOW

Kelsee didn't open her eyes, bracing for the reprimand and anger. Both were as familiar as breathing. She knew how much Alex hated the light shining in his face. She couldn't believe she'd forgotten to close the blinds.

Everything had to be perfect. Always.

When she couldn't take the silence a moment longer, she chanced a peek and released a sigh of relief at the sight of the empty pillow beside her. Then she remembered. He wasn't there. The reason, for the moment, escaped her.

Kelsee snuggled deeper in the sheets and stretched out in the middle of the bed. She tried to relax and reclaim sleep, but her brain was already churning. She couldn't shake the feeling that she'd forgotten something.

The phone rang, and she checked the caller ID screen and groaned. She composed herself before answering, "Hello, Mariam."

Her sister-in-law skipped the usual greeting of 'As-salamu Alaykum' and asked, "Are you ready?"

Kelsee's mind froze. *Ready for what?*

"I can't believe I have to do this." Mariam's usually strong voice cracked.

Memories flooded in. Today was the funeral.

Two days ago, her husband left to play "golf" at the Chandler Park Course in the Five Points area in Atlanta. Kelsee made him a fruit smoothie with spinach and a special ingredient – a hint of mint. He took a sip and mumbled, "Don't want to be late". He poured the rest in a sports bottle and left without saying goodbye.

Kelsee went about her regular Saturday chores of cleaning the house, stripping the sheets, mopping and vacuuming. She was washing their dishes, thinking about what he wanted for their next meal and how much effort it would take to prepare when the phone call came. The call that changed everything.

Her mask firmly in place, Kelsee lied, "I can't believe it either."

She closed her eyes, listening as Mariam sniffed and repeated the same rambling from yesterday. "Why would Allah take him from me so soon? My baby brother. Why?"

Kelsee didn't respond. No one in that family listened to her anyway. Instead, she padded to the bathroom and stared at her reflection in the mirror, wincing at the fresh bruise. A final rebuke from her loving husband.

"Are you listening?" Mariam asked.

Kelsee clenched her jaw against what she really wanted to say. "Of course."

"I said, I'm sending some brothers from the mosque to drive you to the funeral. I'll meet you there. I know things are happening quickly and I appreciate you for following the customs."

Yes, Kelsee knew the customs. Unlike her husband, she studied the faith and used it to her advantage. Custom dictated a quick burial without a viewing. She thought she would at least get to see the body. Mariam handled everything.

"We need to get there at ten," Mariam continued. "The last thing I need on a day like today is to be stuck in I-85 traffic."

Kelsee ended the call and mentally prepared herself to play the part of the grieving widow. Make-up would camouflage the bruise. Dark shades would hide any other remnants of what had become of their marriage. Or maybe she'd display what he'd done. This was one secret he wouldn't take to the grave.

CHAPTER TWO

THREE YEARS AGO

"Are you okay?" Kelsee turned at the sound of Connie's voice. Her friend and fellow nurse had found her outside the Red Zone, the area in the ER where the trauma patients are taken. The team had finished caring for the last victim from a three-car pileup. Two of the victims were children with severe pelvic fractures.

Kelsee hated this part of her job. She tore off the blue paper cloth she wore over her scrubs and tossed it into a silver bin, along with the hair cover and paper booties. She wiped the sweat from her brow and took a deep breath. The coppery smell of blood and pungent scent of fear threatened to take her back to that fateful night years ago when everything changed.

She shook it off and turned to her friend. "I'm good."

Connie studied her face for a moment, peering at her with eyes the color of chestnuts. "Are you sure? I was buried in triage with that accident, but I was worried about you."

"I'm fine." Kelsee managed a smile she didn't feel. "Think we can get in a quick break?"

"That's another reason I came to find you. Guess who's back?" Connie bounced on her toes and raised her eyebrows. Her heart-shaped face held an expression that screamed of mischief.

Kelsee knew that look. Her friend was playing matchmaker again. Any eligible young man who landed in the ER was a target. "You need to stop."

Connie grabbed her arm and led her around a crowd of interns blocking the elevators. The constant beeping, sirens, and hum of hundreds of conversations were giving her a

headache. She'd been in constant motion since arriving at 3 p.m. A glance at her watch showed she still had roughly five hours to go on a twelve-hour shift.

"Officer Williams has been asking for you," Connie said, in an almost breathy whisper. "He's such a nice guy."

Leave it to Connie to get a name. Kelsee preferred to ignore the man whenever he came into the ER. The cop, with the chiseled features and sexy smile, had a habit of trying to coax a reaction from her.

She never obliged.

Kelsee had convinced herself that she didn't need the distraction. Past experience had taught her that most men weren't worth the trouble anyway.

Officer Williams stood at the other end of the corridor. The fluorescent lighting did nothing to dim the attraction she could feel even from this distance. He winked and unleashed that deadly smile.

Kelsee turned away so she wouldn't have to turn down his offer of a drink again. Connie would have a conniption and end up in the psychiatric wing.

"It seems to be quiet now," Kelsee began. "I just want to find an empty room and close my eyes for a minute. Maybe use the bathroom."

Connie's eye widened. "Why did you say that? You know that means we're about to get slammed again."

"You've watched too many episodes of Grey's Anatomy," Kelsee's response was cut off by the squawk of the internal radio at the nursing station.

"Incoming male nineteen, GSW. Chest, likely abdomen. ETA ten minutes."

GSW, gunshot wound victim. The familiar rush of adrenaline coursed through Kelsee's veins. Everyone shifted into action at once. An empty trauma bay was prepped. Vital signs were communicated to the staff. A nurse called ahead to the OR surgeon.

Kelsee joined the staff who gathered around the gurney at the emergency entrance. When the ambulance screamed into the bay, Kelsee sprang forward. Thoughts of Officer Williams were replaced with helping the patient who, from her experience, had a ninety-five percent chance of surviving if his heart was still beating.

What happened next was a blur. She remembered cutting off the patient's clothing without slicing through the bullet holes. She remembered a loud banging sound coming from the admitting area. She remembered the doctor turning toward the hall and screaming. Kelsee could not focus on the male teenager standing in the doorway. All she could recall was the shape of the gun he pointed at her.

* * *

Kelsee came to on a cot. For a blissful two seconds, she didn't know where she was. Her memory returned in waves. The gunshot victim.

The controlled chaos of the emergency room. The smell of sulfur from the gunpowder. A blast of repeated shots, the sound of people falling to the floor.

"I knew I would get you in bed, but I didn't envision it happening this way," a baritone voice said.

Her eyes snapped open. Officer Williams' dark hooded eyes lasered into her own. Up close, she noticed a scar under his clean-shaven chin and his scent, a heady blend of musk cologne.

"What happened?" Kelsee croaked. She swallowed hard and tried to sit up but couldn't navigate the mechanics of her body.

He extended his hand. "Some punk tried to finish off your patient. My partner had to put him down."

"Did anyone on staff get hurt?" Kelsee's insides took a tumble as nerves ran amuck. Nausea threatened when she stood beside him. She didn't think it was because he towered over her. At 5'4", she looked up to most people.

He shook his head. "The security guard at the entrance got hit in the shoulder. A few bumps and bruises from the scramble to safety. And the doctor with dreads…."

Kelsee released the breath she was holding and wiped her hands down the length of her scrubs. "The doctor I was standing beside? Doctor Carter?"

"He took one in the leg but he'll be okay. I'm sorry this happened to you."

She didn't know what to say to that. She was relieved that no one died but the shock of it all brought up painful memories. Kelsee suppressed the feeling of helplessness that threaten to overwhelm her. It was her favorite coping mechanism. Time to get back to work. Kelsee turned to leave and winced from a jab in her side.

"You may feel that for a while," he said, "I had to tackle you."

She grinned unable to recall the moment. "I didn't even get dinner first." Kelsee blinked in horror. Was she really flirting with the man right now?

"I mean, I owe you a thank you."

"I'm Alex, by the way." He cleared his throat. "This may not be an appropriate time but … how about we get a coffee or something?" He tucked a stray curl behind her ear. "As you can see, I'm a nice guy. You have to say yes this time."

His touch fought for space in the jumble of thoughts clouding her mind. She hadn't been on a date since the disastrous affair with a former patient that came in with a severe case of heartburn. Turns out dude really didn't have a heart and she was the one that felt the burn.

"This really isn't the best time to ask for a date, you know." Kelsee took a step back.   Alex hung his head and peered down at her with a raised brow. If this was his idea of an apology, Kelsee thought it was adorable.

Kelsee sighed, allowing his logic – or lack thereof – to sink in. Maybe she should give

Mr. Nice Guy a chance. Before she could respond, Connie burst into the room. "Oh my God, Kelsee," she cried and ran to Kelsee's side. "I was looking everywhere for you."

"I'm right here, Connie." She reassured her friend.

Alex's face transformed from amused to aggravated. The movement was so fast Kelsee wondered if she had imagined it. Before it could fully register, Connie wrapped her in a hug so tight Kelsee flinched and pulled away.

"That was crazy. The whole ER is a crime scene." She leaned in and whispered. "He saved your life. You have to talk to him now."

And she did. Officer Alex was her real-life hero. Someone had finally arrived on time. Kelsee thought she would never have a reason to be afraid again.

She was wrong.

CHAPTER THREE

HIS SECRET

Alex Williams sat on the passenger side of the patrol car watching the towering buildings of downtown Atlanta go by. His partner of five years, Maxwell Collins, drove with one beefy arm hanging out of the window. The balmy fall night air felt good blowing through the open windows.

They were two hours away from the end of an uneventful shift and Alex smiled. He would see her soon.

"What you so damn happy about, youngster?" Max asked.

Alex adjusted the seatbelt and turned to his friend. "When's too soon to get married?"

"Man, she got you wide open." Max laughed as he stopped at a red light.

"I'm serious," Alex said. "I'm ready to lock it down." He had never fallen this hard or this fast for a woman. Kelsee consumed his thoughts even when he didn't want her to.

Max maneuvered through the intersection and scratched his head. "Speaking as someone with two ex-wives, a girlfriend and a friend with benefits, I say it's never too soon for love."

"Would you quit playing?" Alex said with a chuckle. "I'm making life decisions over here."

"Alright, alright." Max pulled into a gas station and cut off the engine. "Listen. Only you'll know if it's right. If you want my opinion, though, Kelsee's a nice girl."

Alex nodded. He valued his partner's input. They may have been total opposites – Max was white and divorced with three kids. Alex was a single, Black Muslim and almost twenty years his junior. But Alex knew he was ready. He was twenty-seven, advancing in a job he loved, and he had found his one.

"You know what makes Kelsee special?" Alex said shifting in the seat. "We've been dating for over nine months and she hasn't once asked me to quit the force."

Alex knew that was a rare thing. All the guys, Max included, talked about how their significant others wanted them to find another job. Everyone wasn't equipped to love someone who put their lives in danger.

Max nodded. "That's special, right there. Misses Number One wanted me to quit before I had to kill somebody. Misses Number Two wanted somebody to kill me."

"Man, you're crazy." Alex laughed, and his friend joined in.

"But seriously," Max said turning to Alex. "If you got someone that understands the job is a calling, a part of who you are, you hold on to that woman."

Alex knew Max was right. He also knew his sister, Mariam, wouldn't approve because Kelsee didn't share their faith. Alex shook his head He wouldn't let his sister bring him down. He didn't need her permission.

He took a deep breath. "I'm going to do it."

"Great," Max slapped his shoulder. "And I'm going to take a leak."

Alex watched his partner's back as he went into the store and spoke to the clerk. He scanned the parking lot more out of habit than genuine concern. They made frequent stops at this station. A green, late model Chrysler pulled up and a young woman got out to pump gas. He could see her kids playing in in the back seat.

He wondered what Kelsee was doing at this moment. They had plans to hook up when he got off work. Alex knew she would have something hot and ready for him and he wasn't thinking about food.

Alex couldn't stop his thoughts from replaying the lustful and passion filled night before. And the night before that. Kelsee's small luscious body fit perfectly against his frame. It wasn't just that the woman was fine. And she was fine. But Kelsee was sexy without even trying. It was her eyes that drew Alex in. They were deep brown pools of need with a hint of something he couldn't name along the edges.

Movement to the left caught Alex's attention. Young black male, about 5'7", baggy jeans, and a black hoodie pulled up to obscure his face. Alex didn't want to automatically assume the guy was a perp. He was sensitive to the community's view of harassment. The guy could be simply going to purchase snacks. But he got out of the car and watched the guy over the roof of the car.

The guy noticed the police car and froze. He raised both hands. "I ain't tripping."

"We good then," Alex responded.

Alex watched Max and the clerk at the counter. He could tell that Max was scoping out the guy the minute he walked in. Max stayed inside until the hoodie guy made his purchases and left.

As soon as they returned to the car, the radio squawked, "Signal 58." Domestic violence call. The address was a familiar one in the Five Points neighborhood. They were a few blocks away, so Alex responded that they were on the way.

They screamed to a stop in front of the house and Alex was out of the car before Max could put it in park.

"I told Bob what would happen if we had to come back here," Alex yelled back at Max.

"Slow down, man. Follow procedure," Max instructed.

All Alex heard was the blood racing through his veins. The front door was ajar and before Alex hit the first step a half-dressed woman jumped out. She was followed closely by her husband.

Alex didn't think. He tackled Bob and started pounding him. Bob's face blurred and became someone else. With every blow, he rained down fury on his father.

"Are you trying to blow it?" Max asked him. They were back in the car outside the scene. "I had to pull you off the guy before you killed him."

"I warned him," Alex said watching the EMS workers put Bob on a stretcher. "I told him if we had to come here again it wouldn't be good for him."

Max opened the car door. "Don't worry about it. The guy was resisting arrest from what I saw. Besides, he was chasing his wife with a knife."

Alex massaged his bruised knuckles. He didn't even register the weapon when he attacked. That could have been a fatal error, but he didn't care. Alex couldn't explain what came over him.

Max exited the vehicle and talked to the other officers milling around the scene. Alex stayed put and nursed his anger. How could a man beat the woman he's supposed to love?

All he knew was the anger felt as familiar as breathing. Alex took several deep breaths and was able to calm down. He would have to cancel on Kelsee tonight. She knew about his past, but he couldn't let her see the violence that coursed through his DNA.

CHAPTER FOUR

HIS SISTER

Alex proposed before introducing Kelsee to his sister. For a while, she thought he was either ashamed of her, or of them as a couple. When they walked into Mariam's bungalow, she realized the issue was something else entirely.

"Sister." Alex greeted the woman standing at the wooden front door with a kiss on both of her flabby cheeks. "How you doing?"

Mariam playfully pushed him away. "Like you care. I haven't heard from you in a week."

"I've been busy." Alex wrapped an arm around Kelsee waist. "I want you to meet my fiancée."

Mariam's light brown gaze flickered with disgust before giving Kelsee a once-over that sent chills down her spine. "What are you talking about? When did this happen?"

Kelsee had thought ripped skinny jeans, bright blue wedge sandals and striped tank top were a cute casual look for lunch with her sister-in-law but based on Mariam's simple black dress and matching hijab, she was wrong.

"We made it official this weekend. Now, are you going to let us in?" Alex motioned for Kelsee to show off the ring.

Mariam pursed her lips but stepped aside to let them in.

Kelsee grabbed Alex's hand and drew the strength to walk into the house but felt the heat from Mariam's glare the entire time. The small space was sparsely decorated with a tan cloth couch, end table, and floor lamp. One wall

housed an overstuffed bookcase. The coffee table was covered with photos of Alex at various stages of life. The centerpiece was a family portrait taken when Alex was missing several teeth. Their father was not in the picture.

Kelsee and Alex settled on the sofa as Mariam disappeared into the kitchen.

"Have I told you today how beautiful you look?" Alex asked, leaning close to Kelsee.

Kelsee could only nod. She wanted Alex's sister to like her and she didn't get the feeling it would be easy.

"Don't worry," Alex said. "I love you. Big Sis will, too."

"Maybe I should go help her." Kelsee was on her feet before she finished the sentence. Her stomach tensed at the thought of being alone with Mariam, but she wanted to do something to lighten the mood. Besides, this was a happy occasion, right?

Alex took the opportunity to smack her ass. "That's my girl."

Kelsee's nerves remained on edge as she made her way to the kitchen threshold. At first, Mariam didn't notice Kelsee standing in the doorway. She peered in the quaint kitchen with all white appliances and cabinets to match. There wasn't a crumb or stain to be found. Mariam shut the refrigerator door with her hip and turned to see Kelsee standing there.

"I … I … wanted to see if you needed any help," Kelsee said.

Mariam shooed her away with a flick of her thick wrists. "I'm sure you don't know the proper way to handle a Muslim meal. Go sit down somewhere."

Kelsee bit back a snide comment. She wouldn't make a scene for Alex's sake, but she was done being intimated by this woman. Kelsee may not have been a Muslim, she didn't even go to church, but she loved Alex. That should be good enough.

The meal was excellent. Kelsee hadn't tried fried ginger fish and mixed vegetables. She relaxed, watching Mariam dote on her brother; fixing his plate, serving him first. Kelsee could picture them as children. That made her realize they both loved this man.

"So, how did you two meet?" Mariam poured more sweet tea in Alex's glass before settling in her chair.

Alex wiped his mouth with the linen napkin. "At work. Well, at the ER where Kelsee works."

He then launched into the story of saving her from the gun-toting teenager. Kelsee had heard this story a hundred times but she could tell from Mariam's straight back and crossed arms that she was not amused. Kelsee gave Alex a nudge with her foot, but he would not be denied his hero story or a moment to shine.

"And that's how I got a date out of her." Alex concluded his tale by leaning over and kissing Kelsee. "I only had to save her life."

Kelsee didn't have to turn toward Mariam to feel the woman's eyes boring into her.

"Isn't that something?" Mariam said with a dry tone pushing away from the table.

"I forgot to tell you. Daisha asked about you."

Kelsee's ears perked up. *Who is Daisha?*

Alex shifted in his chair and cleared his throat. "Oh yeah. Tell her I'm doing good. I'm getting married."

He winked at Kelsee and stroked her leg under the table.

Mariam released a heavy sigh then refocused on Alex. "Don't forget I need you to take a look at my car before you go."

Alex's eyebrows drew in and creased his face. "You trying to rush us on out or something?"

"Of course not," she replied, and her tone softened. "You can do that while Kelsee and I handle the cleanup."

Kelsee could sense the reason Mariam wanted Alex out of the house and it had nothing to do with low tire pressure. The woman had something to say and it wouldn't be something Alex would appreciate. Kelsee reassured Alex with a pointed look.

Alex went into the garage but still looked over one shoulder before he hit the threshold.

CHAPTER FIVE

HIS FAMILY

Kelsee gathered both of their plates and scrapped the remaining food into the trash. Mariam practically snatched the dishes from Kelsee's hands and placed them in the sink. She turned and crossed her arms, almost glaring at Kelsee as she snapped, "I don't need help with the dishes. I need Alex to stop trying to save the world."

Kelsee took a step back. "What?"

"I know my brother, so what's your story?" she snarled. "He may have 'saved' you in that hospital, but what's your real deal? What kind of drama will you bring?"

"I don't know what you're talking about," Kelsee shot back, putting some distance between them. "Are you upset about the way we met, or that he's marrying a non-Muslim?"

Mariam slid a look towards the doorway and took a deep breath. "I'm upset that Alex puts himself in harm's way on purpose."

Kelsee cocked her head and said, "I'm still drawing a blank here. He's a cop. That's kind of the job description."

"Sit down." Mariam gestured to the kitchen table. She glanced at the garage door and walked over to push it shut. "I'm not sure how much of our childhood Alex shared with you."

Kelsee leaned back in the seat. "Enough. I got the highlights." They had told each other about their tragic childhoods one night over pizza and beer. That was the night Kelsee fell in love with Alex.

"Then you know our father was abusive," Mariam took the seat next to Kelsee. "He converted to Islam when I was about five years old.

For all the positive influence the faith had, he didn't change. Alex came nine years later. Mom picked his name because it means 'safety and protection.' All of her prayers couldn't stop Father, though." Mariam picked at a napkin. Her leg bounced as she recalled living in terror every day.

Kelsee reached for Mariam's hand and was surprised she didn't pull away. "You don't have to tell me all this."

"You need to know." Mariam clenched Kelsee's hand. "You need to know that Alex is still that little boy trying to save his mother. Many days he purposefully set Father off so he would spend his rage on him and pass out without hurting Mom."

Kelsee couldn't respond because that was a part of the story she didn't know.

"This happened for years. Until the day, … Father finally went too far and beat her to death. He rots in a jail to this day for what he did." Mariam snarled, "A useless piece of a man." She took a second to compose herself and continued, "I took care of Alex from then on. I was about twenty years old then. No mother. No father. All we had was each other."

"Was Alex there when it happened?" Kelsee asked, knowing she couldn't bring herself to ask him later. She told herself it was to spare him from reliving the pain. In truth, she didn't want to think about watching her own parents die in a horrific accident that night. She'd felt a sense of loss ever since. She and Alex shared the loss of a parent.

Mariam shook her head and released Kelsee's hand. She sat back in the chair. "He was away at camp. Mother tried to keep him involved in any activity that would get him out of the house."

"You think Alex chose to be a policeman to save people because he couldn't save her?"

"I *know* he did. And I know every woman he has been involved with needs to be saved too."

"Even this Daisha you mentioned?" Kelsee's mouth twisted as she said the name.

Alex had said the right thing earlier, but she needed to know if this woman was a threat.

Mariam smiled but there wasn't an ounce of warmth behind it. "No, Daisha is a lovely Muslim woman who would be a better fit for my brother."

"Why? Because she's Muslim?" Kelsee found the concept ridiculous.

"It's because she isn't waiting on someone to save her."

Kelsee blinked. *This woman had a lot of nerve*. She stood. "You don't have to worry about me. That's not my life. Me and Alex are meant for each other."

"So, you think." Mariam pushed herself upright and faced Kelsee. "Because I know my brother. He's a nice guy who doesn't see that some things can't be fixed. You have trouble written all over you."

CHAPTER SIX

HER SECRET

Kelsee tried to shake off the conversation with Mariam during the ride in the car with Alex later that night, but the talk of missing parents had her mind rooted on her own. She leaned against the car door and feigned sleep, so she wouldn't have to answer any questions from Alex about Mariam's talk.

Trouble came for Kelsee on her eighth birthday. She sat in the back seat of her father's prized possession, a black Ford Mustang. Her father, a medium brown man who always had a smile on his face, sang along to the Jackson 5 on the radio while cruising down some back road on the way home from Six Flags Amusement Park. Dad liked to take the long way home because the interstate wasn't scenic enough.

"Come on, Baby K," Dad said. "Hit them background vocals and help me out."

Kelsee perked up and leaned over the bench seat. She took a breath and belted out the lyrics to 'I Want You Back.'

Her Dad loved himself some Motown and Kelsee loved Michael Jackson. He was so cute.

Momma laughed, nudging her father in this side. "You two love to perform."

But she joined in, too.

The family had spent the day at Six Flags, a birthday treat and an award for Kelsee getting straight A's that year. They managed to ride all the attractions that she was tall enough to ride. For the first time, Kelsee got to eat all the junk she wanted. She could barely keep her eyes open, so she didn't say much when Momma made her sit back and buckle up.

She remembered waking up to Momma's scream. The blinding lights and crunch of metal caused Kelsee to cover her eyes and duck her head. The car was lifted in the air, flipped, and crashed back to earth.

Then it was quiet.

Soon, the only sound was the dripping of car fluids and her Momma moaning her name.

Kelsee managed to crawl over the seat. Her dad lay still. He looked like he was asleep except for the steering wheel that was pressed too close to his chest. Blood ran from his nose and covered the lower part of his face and mustache.

Her Mom didn't look much better, but her eyes were open. She managed a smile with half her face. "Are you okay, baby?"

Kelsee tried to nod, but her head was pounding, and she felt waves rolling in her stomach. She climbed into Momma's lap, her small size helping her squeeze into the tight space.

"Momma, I'm scared."

"I know, but Momma needs you to be brave. Can you climb out?" Her words were slow and labored.

"Come with me," Kelsee pleaded.

Momma tried to move but grabbed her leg. Both were pinned under the dashboard.

"You can do it. Tell me what you can see out there. Is anyone around to call for help?"

Kelsee pushed herself up and climbed through the broken glass of the windshield ignoring the sting of cuts on her hands and knees.

The wavy stomach subsided in the cool night air. Kelsee peered through the darkness. All she could make out was a field of trees, a mangled pickup truck, and pieces of metal on the roadway.

Kelsee went back to check on her parents. Dad still wasn't moving, and Momma had her eyes closed. She touched her face. "Momma."

"Did you see anybody, baby?" Her mother's face twisted as she spoke.

"Nobody out there," Kelsee said. "What are we going to do? We need to call 911, right?"

Momma managed a small smile. "Yes, but I guess we have to wait until someone comes and helps us."

Her Momma tried to keep her calm during the wait by stroking her hair and humming songs her father loved.

"Momma," Kelsee whispered, "what if no one comes to save us?"

"Then I want you to do something for me, okay?" she replied, her voice raspy. "You save yourself. Always remember that. You save yourself."

* * *

That night, hours had gone by before Kelsee saw the red and blue lights of an ambulance. Much later, Kelsee would learn that the drunk driver who hit them was thrown from his vehicle and died on the side of the road. Her father died on impact from a crushed chest. Her mother survived the ambulance ride but died on the operating table. Kelsee sustained a traumatic brain injury and some cuts and bruises. Someone had the audacity to say she was lucky.

Kelsee went to live with her maternal grandmother. Rather, she helped take care of the sweet, silver-haired woman. Grandma Sylvia did her best, but she battled arthritis, diabetes, and later, cancer. When she died, Kelsee was sixteen and determined to save people. She arrived at the Carrie-Pitts Children's Home with a game plan. She would take advantage of every available resource and make her mother proud. She would save herself.

Kelsee thought she had done a good job until Alex showed up that day in the ER and showed her what it was like to need saving again.

CHAPTER SEVEN

THE WAY IT WAS

They had been married for a few months before she got a glimpse of the real Alex. Both of their jobs required them to work various shifts, so they tried to sync their schedules to have a least one night off together.

Soon, they settled into the comfortable couple routine of watching the TGIT -Thank God It's Thursday - lineup on ABC. Kelsee would make Alex's favorite dish, bourbon salmon with broccoli and brown rice in the proper preparation that would even appease Mariam.

Alex didn't show up on the evening they were supposed to celebrate the day they met.

Kelsee tried to call, but his cell phone went straight to voicemail. She contacted his precinct but became lost in a tangle of transferred calls.

When he walked in two hours later, Kelsee had worked herself into a frenzy. The dinner was ruined, and she was prepared to let him have the full wrath of her anger.

"Sometimes things come up on the job," he explained. "I pulled over a DUI, which meant extra paperwork. You have to be flexible."

Alex sounded reasonable, but her nasty attitude would not be contained. She stood with her hands on her hips. "You are inconsiderate. I have a demanding job too, but I'm here and even made dinner."

"Smells good too, Babe."

"That's not the point, Alex." Kelsee tried to calm herself by taking deep breaths.

Alex cocked his head. "You okay?"

Kelsee had looked forward to cozying up on the couch with Alex so she could share her news. And he looked so fine standing there in his uniform. She nodded and Alex relaxed.

"I'm here now. Aren't you happy to see me?" Alex went into the bedroom to take off his gear. When he came back, he wore a simple white t-shirt and a pair of gym shorts.

Kelsee was distracted by the sight of his muscular thighs. She forgot all about the silly argument.

Alex sank into the couch and patted the space next to him. "Come here, woman."

Kelsee went to him and he wrapped her in his arms. "I think I asked you a question. You happy to see me or what?"

Instead of answering, Kelsee kissed him. They stayed locked in a sensual, intimate embrace while Alex's tongue teased and explored her mouth and her neck. A moan escaped from Kelsee and Alex maneuvered her body until she straddled his lap. The cotton fabric of Alex's shorts could not contain his need.

He peeled off her clothes and Kelsee lost herself in the feel of Alex's skin against her own. This is when she felt the safest. Wrapped up in Alex, her thoughts at bay, she could focus on gentleness of his touch. He licked and teased her until she felt lightheaded.

When he finally entered her, she cried out his name. With each thrust, she knew that Alex had saved her in more ways than one. She didn't have to be afraid to love him. He wouldn't leave her.

After they were spent and lay in a tangle of limbs, Kelsee whispered her news.

"Are you serious?" Alex's brown eyes danced with joy. "We're having a baby."

She nodded, and he squeezed her tight. "I promise, I'll be a good Dad," he said.

They stayed up all night planning their future family together.

Kelsee remembered being happy. So happy, she forgot about all the heartache in the past. She forgot that some people can't be saved.

And it was her own body that betrayed her this time.

CHAPTER EIGHT

SAVING HER

That was the first miscarriage, but it wouldn't be the last. After each one, Kelsee felt herself spiral down a path of self-destruction and she was determined to take Alex with her.

Every conversation became an argument. Every argument became a reason for Kelsee to push Alex to the dark places in his past.

"You're just like your father!" she screamed at him one night. His offense, he forgot her new work schedule. Kelsee had given up the hectic ER to work a more stable schedule in the Cancer Center. They both thought the slower pace would help one of their babies survive.

They were wrong.

Alex's icy glare stopped her in her tracks. "What did you say to me?" he growled through a tight jaw.

Kelsee didn't recognize this side of Alex. She knew she was getting dangerously close to an unspeakable line, but common sense didn't kick in. "You heard me. You're just like him. A useless piece of a man."

Alex's body tensed. His hands clenched into fists and he was in her face in an instant. His breath was hot as he towered over her. She shook off the panic that threatened to rise. This was her husband. He was the nice guy. She could explain.

"I'm sorry, okay?" she demurred, holding up her hands in surrender. "I've been dealing with these headaches and I'm taking it out on you. Let's go to bed, okay?"

Kelsee tried to squeeze past Alex but he blocked her path and grabbed her arm.

"You don't get to talk to me like that."

She searched his face, but his eyes were cold. He seemed to look right through her. "Alex, please. You're hurting me."

He looked down and appeared surprised that he had a vise grip on her arm. He let her go and stepped back.

Kelsee massaged the spot. She could see the bruise raising on her creamy skin.

"I'm sorry," Alex said. He ran a trembling hand over his face and backed away.

Is this how it starts?

"You're making me crazy," he confessed.

She went to him and took his hands. "Don't give up on me. I need you to help me. You've always been my hero."

Alex nodded and stroked a gentle hand through her hair. "What if I can't save you anymore?"

CHAPTER NINE

THE END

"I don't know if I can take this anymore."

Kelsee didn't know who said it first, but their marriage was crumbling. She felt helpless to fix it.

She would scream and curse Alex until he reacted. Sometimes things would get physical. Kelsee savored those moments the most.

Alex would leave and Kelsee knew he was running to her. Daisha Evans. He said he was going to his sister's house, but Kelsee had followed him one night. He went to his sister's, but the blue Honda Accord belonged to that woman.

Soon, Kelsee no longer recognized her-self. She didn't think she was the type of woman to try counseling, but she went to please Alex. He thought it would help. She lasted two sessions. No one needed to tell her how to fix things. All she needed was Alex. He saved her once. He could save them both if he wanted to.

He didn't want to.

Yet, Kelsee kept trying. The day before he died, he told Kelsee that he couldn't continue living this way. She looked into her husband's eyes and saw that he had already left her. He just hadn't packed his bags yet.

Kelsee wailed and fell to her knees. The tears were a mixture of relief and anxiety that he was no longer alive. Without Alex to tell her who she was, who would she become? Who was she now that she was alone?

His presence and scent were everywhere. Before she could stop herself, she pulled out the cleaning supplies. She stripped the bed and put on fresh sheets. She scrubbed every surface.

Threw away his newspapers and magazines. Boxed up his awards and plaques. Removed the pictures. And when she was sweaty and weary, Kelsee took a shower and climbed into the middle of the bed.

Sleep was an elusive concept. She couldn't get rid of the nagging notion that she was forgetting something.

CHAPTER TEN

BACK TO NOW

Kelsee had one more performance to get through.

Connie accompanied her to the memorial.

The funeral home was a modest brick building with dreary gray carpeting, muted lighting and an aerosol scent of cleaning products. A few flowers lined the closed casket up front. Several police officers milled around whispering among themselves.

She walked to the front and sat in the velvet lined pew. Her sister-in-law marched out of a room in the back and sat on the other side of the aisle.

"Is that Mariam?" Connie asked. "Why isn't she sitting with you?"

Kelsee shrugged. "She never liked me. I guess she doesn't have to pretend anymore."

The doors opened and Kelsee turned to see who else had joined the ceremony. She almost fell out the pew when Daisha paraded down the aisle and took the space next to Mariam.

She couldn't believe that woman had the nerve to show up. She had taken Alex from her when he was alive. Did she have to come and disrespect her here, too?

Two could play that game.

Kelsee removed her shades, but Mariam refused to look her way.

The service started with a prayer and then a Muslim minister cleared his throat. "Since our Brother Alex was an Officer of the Law, I'm going to do things a little different. Would anyone like to say a few words?"

Kelsee scanned those in attendance. This was going differently than she imagined. No one stirred.

Connie leaned over to Kelsee. "Are you going to say anything?"

She shook her head. She wasn't prepared to talk about her husband.

Finally, a policeman came forward. Kelsee recognized Alex's partner, Max, as he went to the podium.

"I can't believe we are gathered here today," Max began, his pudgy cheeks hung low. "Alex has been my partner for several years. We had some good times. I could always count on him, you know. He always had my back. It doesn't seem right that someone that young would have a heart attack."

Kelsee shook her head. Working in the medical profession, she knew that some things couldn't be explained. Parents die in car accidents, babies die in the womb. Even healthy husbands could suddenly pass away.

"I mean, I couldn't get past that fact," Max admitted. "And I know it goes against the culture, but Mariam gave me the go ahead. I had the coroner do a toxic screen."

"What?" Kelsee didn't realize she had verbalized her thought until everyone turned to look at her.

Mariam glared at her and Daisha had a weird expression on her face. Kelsee wondered what was going on.

"Like I was saying," Max continued. "I just couldn't get past it. Alex was one of the good guys, you know. He had a loving wife and sister. And I hope it will bring some comfort to know that I got the report right before I got here."

Beads of sweat formed on Kelsee's forehead. She grabbed a paper fan from the seat next to her and tried to cool off.

Max retrieved a piece of paper out of his pocket and made a production of unfolding it. He smoothed it on the podium and looked up.

"Seems as if Alex had traces of a drug called Taxol in his system."

He paused, letting the information echo in the room.

"This drug is used to treat breast cancer survivors." Max tucked the paper back into his pocket. "Now, for the life of me, I can't imagine why Alex would have that in his system so I decided to ask him."

Kelsee's mind was racing, and she almost missed Max's last comments. A gasp from Connie made her look up.

Alex stood there.

"What …what's going on?" Kelsee stammered bracing herself in the pew.

Alex held up a vial and tilted his head to look at it. "Hey, Babe. You forgot something, didn't you?"

Now Kelsee remembered the thing that had been nagging at her for the past two days. When she was cleaning last night, she didn't go into the pantry. Hidden away behind the spices and seasoning was the bottle she took from inventory at work.

"You can't be here," Kelsee said. "They called and told me you died. I watched you drink it. I mean, you took it with you. You should have …"

"And that broke my heart," Alex said. "I mean, it would have hurt less if you stabbed me. I knew we were having problems, but I would never hurt you."

Kelsee pointed to her face. "You did hurt me. No one knows the real you."

"You did that to yourself, sweetheart. I knew no one would believe me if I told them you were hitting me. So, I hid cameras in the house. It shows how you tried to provoke me and when I would leave, you would abuse yourself."

How did this happen?

Her chest tightened. "It's your fault," she mumbled.

Kelsee always thought Alex would stop her. She thought they would be able to get past the bitterness and disappointment and find their way back to each other. She didn't think Alex would try to leave her. Not for that woman. Not for anyone.

Everyone that ever left Kelsee died. Why did Alex think he could leave her and live? Kelsee remembered her Mother's final words. *You save yourself.*

She snapped out of her trance when she felt the handcuffs snap on her wrist. Mariam rose and stood by Alex. "We wanted you to know we were onto your scheme. **I** wanted to see your face when they arrested you."

Daisha joined them and placed a possessive hand on Alex's arm. "Don't worry. Alex will be fine."

How did this happen? The crowd seemed to suffocate Kelsee. Connie kept asking her what was going on. Someone started to read her rights. The metal bracelets cut into her skin when she tried to pull free.

"How can you do this to me?" Kelsee cried almost blinded by her tears. "You're supposed to save me. You're the nice guy."

Alex moved forward and leaned in to whisper, "I'm not that nice."

ACKNOWLEDGEMENTS

Thank you so much for reading, *Not That Nice*. If you enjoyed Kelsee and Alex's story, please take a moment to share your thoughts in a short review. I appreciate you for taking the time to do so.

Special thanks go out to my fellow scribes in the NK Tribe Called Success. It takes a village to maintain this writing thing and I am blessed that I found mine.

ABOUT THE AUTHOR

Her pen sharpens spine-tingling tales of betrayal,
lies, consequences…and their fallout when the truth
comes out. Fitting for her brand of literary inspiration
– shining the light in the darkness of deceit.

National Best-selling Author Michelle D. Rayford is
a doting wife, rocking mother and the dynamic CEO
of Barrington Drive Publishing. The seed for
Michelle's gift of storytelling was planted well before she was old enough to drive…now this talented
scribe is driven to INSPIRE. Her red-hot keyboard

has cranked out hits for several anthologies, as well as her soulful debut novel – *Moment of Truth* and the chilling *Not That Nice*. Her latest book, *Settling Up*, is scheduled to come blasting onto reading lists everywhere in 2020.

Michelle's laptop is housed in the colorful south, where she resides with her husband, who she's spent half her life crushing on, and two daughters who push her to keep the dream going. When she's not reading, jamming to her 80's music playlist or playing NBA2K, Michelle is hard at work, hanging out with her vivid imagination, developing stories about the messy parts of relationships and the aftermath of declaring *I do*. She loves chatting with readers and book clubs; reach out to her at mdrayford@gmail.com or through her website - www.michelledrayford.com.

Michelle D. Rayford – driving readers to literary pleasure!

When the cradle breaks the vows…all hell breaks loose.

Adrienne is obsessed with the new man in her life – the bouncing baby boy she's always dreamt of having…over her husband Logan's staunch objections. Motherhood. Wealth. Power. On the surface, the joyful mother has it all – but beneath the bliss, a scandal is brewing that will rip her contentment to shreds.

Logan's professional aspirations leave little room for marriage, family…or guarding his secrets. He's laser focused on surpassing his father's success in the family law firm, and when an affluent new client breezes into town, Logan has one shot to overtake his father…if his wife will get out of his way.

When the past collides with the present, will the truth set Adrienne free?